D1566854

The Legend of the Fairy Stones

written and designed by
Kelly Anne White

NEW YORK

LONDON • NASHVILLE • MELBOURNE • VANCOUVER

The Legend of the Fairy Stones

Published in New York, New York, by Morgan James Publishing. Morgan James is a trademark of Morgan James, LLC. www.MorganJamesPublishing.com.

Published in association with the literary agency of Legacy, LLC, 501 N. Orlando Avenue, Suite #313–348, Winter Park, FL 32789, www.Legacy-Management.com.

The Morgan James Speakers Group can bring authors to your live event. For more information or to book an event visit The Morgan James Speakers Group at www.TheMorganJamesSpeakersGroup.com.

ISBN 9781642791952 paperback
Library of Congress Control Number: 2018951677

Graphic designer: Kelly White
Product developer: Kim Childress
Art coordinator: Jamey Walston
Design consultant: Chun Kim

In an effort to support local communities, raise awareness and funds, Morgan James Publishing donates a percentage of all book sales for the life of each book to Habitat for Humanity Peninsula and Greater Williamsburg.

Get involved today! Visit www.MorganJamesBuilds.com.

Cover art credits:

Virginia State Parks, "Mushrooms," 2012, photo, Flickr

P. B. Abery and Wallace Jones, "Three Fairies," 1909, photo, National Library of Wales

Nicolaas Struyk, "A Dragonfly," early to mid 18th century, pen and black ink and watercolor over touches of graphite, Metropolitan Museum of Art, New York, (bequest of Catherine G. Curran, 2008)

Dedication page credit:

The Children's Museum of Indianapolis, "Roller Skates," photo

To my grand girls Ryland and Lorelei for an Easter treasure hunt that
inspired this book, and of course Lexi—one of my favorite Stones.
(The unicorn is for you, snowy Zoë.) Always with love, Kiki

Midst midnight mist of long ago . . .

Fairies flitted, glittered aglow. Carefree with glee in glens and glades, they played 'til dawn when moonbeams fade. Entranced, they danced in deep delight, in scattered light of morning's might.

As sunrays struck the noontime hour, they lolled in beds of fragrant flower.

Once shades of dusk eclipsed their wings they rose to tend to fairy things as songbirds prayed in trills and swells to tender tunes of tinkle bells.

O blessings a rhythmic melody brings to fairies that sing to harmony's ring

Fairies with mushrooms and fairies that bloom, fairies in costume and fairies on brooms

Fairies that flutter wherever they're led, fairies that tiptoe on spiderweb thread

Fairies of fancy all dolled up just right

Others so bright they illumine the night

Fairies that know how to grow what they sow, fairies that flow like a vortex of snow

Fairies that feel what it is to be free, wading in dreams of gold sand and sweet sea

Fairies that glide

Fairies that hide and the fairies that glance

Fairies with books and some nesting in nooks

Fairies that follow clues through the hollow

Fairies that kiss—smooch!—in bountiful bliss

Fairies with wands, oh!   Or are they batons?

Dear fairy godmothers, sooooooo many others

And then one gloomy doom-filled day came dreadful news from far away.
Trekking from a distant city, sadness sang a somber ditty.

It was indeed so sad but true. The fairies turned to hues of blue.

Yes, Christ had died...been crucified.

The fairies cried.   And cried and cried.

The saddest thing they'd ever heard
they never spoke of, not one word.

You see, they sensed He still was near
so every tear released all fear.

The fairy tears dropped here and there,
but first they lingered in the air.

When teardrops finally hit the ground, they turned to stones. But they weren't round.
Tucked in pads of herbs and mosses, perceived losses turned to crosses!

The cross-shaped stones
on earth's dirt floor
dissolved the grief
forevermore.

Now even after all these years, the forest's full of fairy tears.
Look closely when you're in the woods, as fairy stones are pure and good.
You spot one? Stash it in a sack, for bravery is at your back.

Hear woodland whispers speak to you of nature's wishes.

Fairy stones silence chants of old witches, freeing lost souls of twitches and switches

Fairy stones trip up the trick of the troll, proving deception a pitiful hole

Fairy stones giggle at goblins that drool, lifting the truth to make wise men of fools

Fairy stones lighten what lurks in the shade, only a shadow so don't be afraid

Fairy stones dissipate hauntings of ghosts, strumming at heartstrings of heavenly hosts

Fairy stones snuff out a dragon's scorched breath,
extinguishing fire that's leaping toward death

Fairy stones zoom in on zombies' zapped eyes, inviting to wake, inspiring to rise

Fairy stones vanquish venom of vampires

Unveiling love that is humbler but higher

Fairy stones rub out the reaper's grim task, life everlasting now wholly unmasked

Fairy stones soothe while a devilish tug fails, rapture prevails to transcend rusty nails

For fiendish lies have no real meanings, nor do any daunting demons.

Such knowledge rests in precious parts
of open minds   and happy hearts.

Sheer courage set in solid rock
inspires all to boldly walk

Along a path of certainty that's paved with love so gracefully.

Serving as a hushed reminder, nothing else could be much kinder

Than windblown tones that gently moan, "The legend of the fairy stones."

Canst thy bind the unicorn with his band in the furrow...
or will he harrow the valleys after thee? —Job 39:10 AKJV

Um, Are Fairy Stones for Real?

Kola Peninsula, Russia

You betcha! Fairy stones are the real deal. Cross my heart.

Cross-shaped fairy stones are scientifically known as staurolite crystals. Through a geologic process called cruciform penetration twinning, the stones form naturally over the course of time into spectacular prismatic crosses of varying sizes and compositions.

Fairy Stones' Color Tones

The usually opaque complexions of staurolite range in shades from charcoal gray and rusty brown to darkish yellow or muddy pink. It's been said that fairy stones' spectrum of colors represents the whole human race.

Fairy Stones Are Made of...

Snakeskin, snails, and lizard tails. Just kidding! Staurolite can form from several different types of minerals, depending on the region, to include albite, almandine, biotite, garnet, kyanite, micas, muscovite, paragonite, quartz, sillimanite, tourmaline, and other elements.

Taos, New Mexico

Where in the World?

Minas Gerais, Brazil

Fom Afghanistan to Zimbabwe, about fifty countries have reports of fairy stone finds. Staurolite stones have been discovered across Australia and Austria, within several districts of Brazil, in many provinces of Canada, in prefectures of China, on hills of Finland, near rivers in France, in quarries of Germany, along the gold belt of Ghana, in counties of Ireland, amid valleys of Italy, in communes of Madagascar, inside national parks in Namibia and New Zealand, in parts of Portugal, in regions of Russia, in mines of South Africa and Sweden, and on beaches and near glens in the United Kingdom.

Photo credits: Rob Lavinsky, "Staurolite-26463" and "Staurolite-65715," 2010, iRocks.com; Carptrash,

Where in the States?

In the United States, fairy stones collect around springs and ranges of Georgia, where staurolite is the official state mineral.

Ball Ground, Georgia

(Can you find fairy stones hidden in some pages of this book?)

The crystal crosses gather in dozens of other states as well. Most notably, staurolite is found near creeks in Idaho, at a Native American reservation in Kansas, by a waterfall in Maine, in neighborhoods of Maryland, at a dam in Minnesota, along the river in Mississippi, near lakes in New Hampshire, in canyons of New Mexico, on farmlands of North Carolina, and in the lush foothills of the Blue Ridge Mountains in Virginia, where the rocky crosses that fleck the ground are affectionately referred to as fairy stones.

Stuart, Virginia

And So the Story Goes...

Through oral tradition, storytellers still pass along the enchanting folklore of staurolite crosses forming from fairy tears. In Virginia's Fairy Stone State Park brochures, the legend goes something like this:

Hundreds of years before Pocahontas's father, Chief Powhatan, reined over the land that is now Virginia, fairies danced and played with naiads and wood nymphs around springs of water. One day an elfin messenger arrived from a city far away and brought news of the death of Christ. When the fairies heard the story of the crucifixion, they wept. As their tears fell upon the ground, they crystallized to form beautiful crosses. Historic superstitions held that possessing one of these rare stones would protect its owner from illness and accidents, and even ward off a witch's curse.

This fairy stone jazz went down way before the chief was in charge.

Art Attributions

Deep appreciation is extended to the artists whose works appear in this book—well over one hundred images. Some fall under various Creative Commons licenses through which copyright holders have kindly and generously granted reprint permission, and those are attributed here.

Most of the book's artworks are in the public domain, which typically means the art is too old to be copyrighted. It is a blessing that classic storybook illustrators such as Arthur Rackham, Beatrix Potter, Ida Rentoul Outhwaite, John Bauer, Richard Doyle, and Virginia Frances Sterrett each contributed several pieces of art to this project. Even two paintings by iconic impressionist Vincent van Gogh are featured. I give the most thanks, of course, to our loving God.

For complete image credits on *The Legend of the Fairy Stones*, visit KellyAnneWhite.com.

Page 16–17, cont.
VxD, "Frogs," 2006, drawing, Wikimedia Commons

Annett Silbermann, "Fox," 2018, photo, Wikimedia Commons

Beatrix Potter, "Mycological Illustration of the Reproductive System of a Fungus, Hygrocybe Coccinea," 1897, watercolor, The Armitt Museum

Virginia Frances Sterrett, "They Were Three Months Passing through the Forest," illustration from *Old French Fairy Tales*, written by Comtesse de Ségur, (Philadelphia: The Penn Publishing Company, 1920), 60, University of California

Page 19
Jay Ouellet, "Twinkle-Twinkle," 2007, photo

Page 23
Starline, "Blue Comic Background with Lines and Halftone," 2017, digital art, Freepik.com

Kabir Bakie, "Jesus Crucifixion," photo, 2004, Wikimedia Commons

Page 24
phanie fanette, "Friendly Space," digital art, Vecteezy.com

Page 26
Wolf Bubenik, "Staurolith-T2-M3-M4-Layer," 2007, digital art, Wikimedia Commons

Rob Lavinsky, "Staurolite-247852," 2010, photo, iRocks.com

Page 27
Virginia State Parks, "You Looking at ME?," 2011, photo, Flickr

Page 30
Mariana Ruiz Villarreal, "DnD Goblin," 2017, digital art, Wikimedia Commons

Page 31
brionv, "Awaiting the Feast," 2011, photo, Flickr

"Shadow Person," 2006, photo, CopyrightFreePhotos.hq101.com

Page 32
Bonnybbx, "Female Spirit on a Street," 2015, digital art, Wikimedia Commons

Eugenia, "Warrior on the Bottom," 2013, photo, Wikimedia Commons

Page 34
Christian Berry, "Dracula Chess," 2007, digital art, Wikimedia Commons

Virginia State Parks, "Zombie Run Logo," 2014, digital art, Flickr

Page 35
Pexels, "Cloudy Dark Full Moon," 2016, photo, Pixabay.com

J. Scott Altenbach, "A Little Brown Myotis Is in Flight," photo, Bat Conservation International

Magnus Hagdorn, "Newington Cemetery," 2017, photo, Flickr

Page 37
320d, "Rusted Nails," 2015, photo, Wikimedia Commons

Page 38
Derek Horton, "King Kong Statue," 2016, photo, Wikimedia Commons

Dmitry Khrapovitsky, armandeo64.deviantart.net, "Goblin," 2009, digital art, Wikimedia Commons

feraliminal, "Werewolf," 2010, digital art, Wikimedia Commons

Page 39
Vsion, "Be Kind," 2005, digital art, Wikimedia Commons

Joaquim Alves Gaspar, "Gate to Heavens," 2015, photo, Wikimedia Commons

Page 40
Observer Media Group, "Fairies Take Flight at Historic Spanish Point," 2015, photo, YourObserver.com

Richard Doyle, "Triumphal March of the Elf King," illustration from *In Fairy-Land* by Richard Doyle, (London: Longmans, Green, Reader, and Dyer, 1870), 15, University of Florida

Page 41
John Bauer, illustration for "Sagan om de fyra Stortrollen och Lille Vill-Vallareman" by Cyrus Granér in *Among Gnomes and Trolls*, (Åhlén & Åkerlunds förlag, 1909), Wikimedia Commons

"The sun says his prayers," said the fairy.
Or else he would wither and die.

"The sun says his prayers," said the fairy,
"For strength to climb up through the sky.

He leans on invisible angels,
And faith is his prop and his rod.

The sky is his crystal cathedral.

And dawn is his altar to God."

—Vachel Lindsay (1879–1931)

About the Author

Kelly Anne White is author of *The Bible Adventure Book of Scavenger Hunts* and other books for children, teens, and young adults. Kelly has edited and contributed to hundreds of books in nearly every genre for HarperCollins, Kirkus Media, and Christian Editor Connection. Prior to her ventures into book publishing, Kelly spent fifteen years near the tippy-top of the masthead as executive editor of *Girls' Life* magazine. She is an instructor for The PEN Institute and a lesson designer on SchoolhouseTeachers.com. Kelly is on staff at the central Enoch Pratt Free Library, and she conducts professional studies courses at Morgan State University. Kelly lives in Baltimore, Maryland, and enjoys weekends on Chincoteague Bay in Virginia.

CPSIA information can be obtained
at www.ICGtesting.com
Printed in the USA
LVHW071658090519
617262LV00017B/375/P